KERFOL

BY

EDITH WHARTON

British Library Cataloguing-in-Publication Data
A catalogue record for this book is available from the
British Library

Edith Wharton

Edith Wharton was born in New York City in 1862. Her family were extremely wealthy, and during her youth she was provided private tuition and travelled extensively in Europe. A voracious reader, Wharton studied literature, philosophy, science, and art, and began to write poetry and short fiction. In 1885, aged 23, Edith married a banker, Edward Robbins, and for the next few years they travelled extensively together. Living near Central Park in New York, Wharton's first poems were published in *Scribner's Magazine*. In 1891, the same publication printed the first of her many short stories, titled 'Mrs. Manstey's View'. Over the next four decades, they – along with other well-established American publications such as *Atlantic Monthly*, *Century Magazine*, *Harper's* and *Lippincott's* – regularly published her work.

A lifelong keen architect, in 1902 Wharton designed and built her home, The Mount, in Lenox, Massachusetts. It was while living here that she wrote many of her works, including the 1905 novel *The House of Mirth*, which was that year's bestseller, and is now considered a classic of American literary Naturalism. In the period leading up to the First World War, Wharton wrote prolifically, and in 1921 she received the Pulitzer Prize – the first ever woman to do so – for her novel *The Age of Innocence*. Like much of her work, the novel examines the tension between societal pressures and the pursuit of genuine happiness, and includes careful use of dramatic irony.

Edith Wharton died of a stroke in 1937, aged 75. In addition to her novels, she is remembered for her short fiction, especially her excellent ghost stories.

I.

"You ought to buy it," said my host; "its Just the place for a solitary-minded devil like you. And it would be rather worth while to own the most romantic house in Brittany. The present people are dead broke, and it's going for a song—you ought to buy it."

It was not with the least idea of living up to the character my friend Lanrivain ascribed to me (as a matter of fact, under my unsociable exterior I have always had secret yearnings for domesticity) that I took his hint one autumn afternoon and went to Kerfol. My friend was motoring over to Quimper on business: he dropped me on the way, at a cross-road on a heath, and said: "First turn to the right and second to the left. Then straight ahead till you see an avenue. If you meet any peasants, don't ask your way. They don't understand French, and they would pretend they did and mix you up. I'll be back for you here by sunset—and don't forget the tombs in the chapel."

I followed Lanrivain's directions with the hesitation occasioned by the usual difficulty of remembering whether he had said the first turn to the right and second to the left, or the contrary. If I had met a peasant I should certainly have asked, and probably been sent astray; but I had the desert landscape to myself, and so stumbled on the right turn and walked across the heath till I came to an avenue. It was so unlike any other avenue I have ever seen that I instantly knew it must be *the* avenue. The grey-trunked trees sprang up straight to a great height and then interwove their pale-grey branches in a long tunnel through which the autumn light fell faintly. I know most trees by name, but I haven't to this day been able to decide what those trees were. They had the tall curve of elms, the tenuity of poplars, the ashen colour of olives under a rainy sky; and they stretched ahead of me for half a mile or more without a break in their arch. If ever I saw an avenue that unmistakably led to something, it was the avenue at Kerfol. My heart beat a little as I began to walk down it.

Presently the trees ended and I came to a fortified gate in a long wall. Between me and the wall was an open space of grass, with other grey avenues radiating from it. Behind the wall were tall slate roofs mossed with silver, a chapel belfry, the top of a keep. A moat filled with wild shrubs and brambles surrounded the place; the drawbridge had been replaced by a stone arch, and the portcullis by an iron gate. I stood for a long time on the hither side of the moat, gazing about me, and letting the influence of the place sink in. I said to myself: "If I wait long enough, the guardian will turn up and show me the tombs—" and I rather hoped he wouldn't turn up too soon.

I sat down on a stone and lit a cigarette. As soon as I had done it, it struck me as a puerile and portentous thing to do, with that great blind house looking down at me, and all the empty avenues converging on me. It may have been the depth of the silence that made me so conscious of my gesture. The squeak of my match sounded as loud as the scraping of a brake, and I almost fancied I heard it fall when I tossed it onto the grass. But there was more than that: a sense of irrelevance, of littleness, of futile bravado, in sitting there puffing my cigarette-smoke into the face of such a past.

I knew nothing of the history of Kerfol—I was new to Brittany, and Lanrivain had never mentioned the name to me till the day before—but one couldn't as much as glance at that pile without feeling in it a long accumulation of history. What kind of history I was not prepared to guess: perhaps only that sheer weight of many associated lives and deaths which gives a majesty to all old houses. But the aspect of Kerfol suggested something more—a perspective of stern and cruel memories stretching away, like its own grey avenues, into a blur of darkness.

Certainly no house had ever more completely and finally broken with the present. As it stood there, lifting its proud roofs and gables to the sky, it might have been its own funeral monument. "Tombs in the chapel? The whole place is a tomb!" I reflected. I hoped more and more that the guardian would not come. The details of the place, however striking, would seem trivial compared with its collective impressiveness; and I wanted only to sit there and be penetrated by the weight of its silence.

"It's the very place for you!" Lanrivain had said; and I was overcome by the almost blasphemous frivolity of suggesting to any living being that Kerfol was the place for him. "Is it possible that any one could *not* See—?" I wondered. I did not finish the thought: what I meant was undefinable. I stood up and wandered toward the gate. I was beginning to want to know more; not to *see* more—I was by now so sure it was not a question of seeing—but to feel more: feel all the place had to communicate. "But to get in one will have to rout out the keeper," I thought reluctantly, and hesitated. Finally I crossed the bridge and tried the iron gate. It yielded, and I walked through the tunnel formed by the thickness of the *chemin de ronde.* At the farther end, a wooden barricade had been laid across the entrance, and beyond it was a court enclosed in noble architecture. The main building faced me; and I now saw that one half was a mere ruined front, with gaping windows through which the wild growths of the moat and the trees of the park were visible. The rest of the house was still in its robust beauty. One end abutted on the round tower, the other on the small traceried chapel, and in an angle of the building stood a graceful well-head crowned with mossy urns. A few roses grew against the walls, and on an upper window-sill I remember noticing a pot of fuchsias.

My sense of the pressure of the invisible began to yield

to my architectural interest. The building was so fine that I felt a desire to explore it for its own sake. I looked about the court, wondering in which corner the guardian lodged. Then I pushed open the barrier and went in. As I did so, a dog barred my way. He was such a remarkably beautiful little dog that for a moment he made me forget the splendid place he was defending. I was not sure of his breed at the time, but have since learned that it was Chinese, and that he was of a rare variety called the "Sleeve-dog." He was very small and golden brown, with large brown eyes and a ruffled throat: he looked like a large tawny chrysanthemum. I said to myself: "These little beasts always snap and scream, and somebody will be out in a minute."

The little animal stood before me, forbidding, almost menacing: there was anger in his large brown eyes. But he made no sound, he came no nearer. Instead, as I advanced, he gradually fell back, and I noticed that another dog, a vague rough brindled thing, had limped up on a lame leg. "There'll be a hubbub now," I thought; for at the same moment a third dog, a long-haired white mongrel, slipped out of a doorway and joined the others. All three stood looking at me with grave eyes; but not a sound came from them. As I advanced they continued to fall back on muffled paws, still watching me. "At a given point, they'll all charge at my ankles: it's one of the jokes that dogs who live together put up on one," I thought. I was not alarmed, for they were neither large nor formidable. But they let me wander about the court as I pleased, following me at a little distance—always the same distance—and always keeping their eyes on me. Presently I looked across at the ruined facade, and saw that in one of its empty window-frames another dog stood: a white pointer with one brown ear. He was an old grave dog, much more experienced than the others; and he seemed to be observing me with a deeper intentness. "I'll hear from *him*," I said to myself; but he stood in the window-frame, against the trees of the park, and continued to watch me without moving. I stared back at him for a time, to see if the sense that he was being watched would not rouse him. Half the width of the court lay between us, and we gazed at each other silently across it. But he did not stir, and at last I turned away. Behind me I found the rest of the pack, with a newcomer added: a small black greyhound with pale agate-coloured eyes. He was shivering a little, and his expression was more timid than that of the others. I noticed that he kept a little behind them. And still there was not a sound.

I stood there for fully five minutes, the circle about me—waiting, as they seemed to be waiting. At last I went up to the little golden-brown dog and stooped to pat him. As I did so, I heard myself give a nervous laugh. The little dog did not start, or growl, or take his eyes from me—he simply slipped back about a yard, and then paused and continued to look at me. "Oh, hang it!" I exclaimed, and walked across the court toward the well.

As I advanced, the dogs separated and slid away into different corners of the court. I examined the urns on the well, tried a locked door or two, and looked up and down the dumb façade; then I faced about toward the chapel. When I turned I perceived that all the dogs had disappeared except the old pointer, who still watched me from the window. It was rather a relief to be rid of that cloud of witnesses; and I began to look about me for a way to the back of the house. "Perhaps there'll be somebody in the garden," I thought. I found a way across the moat, scrambled over a wall smothered in brambles, and got into the garden. A few lean hydrangeas and geraniums pined in the flower-beds, and the ancient house looked down on them indifferently. Its garden side was plainer and severer than the other: the long granite front, with its few windows and steep roof, looked like a fortress-prison. I walked around the farther wing, went up some disjointed steps, and entered the deep twilight of a narrow and incredibly old box-walk. The walk was just wide enough for one person to slip through, and its branches met overhead. It was like the ghost of a box-walk, its lustrous green all turning to the shadowy greyness of the avenues. I walked on and on, the branches hitting me in the face and springing back with a dry rattle; and at length I came out on the grassy top of the *chemin de ronde*. I walked along it to the gate-tower, looking down into the court, which was just below me. Not a human being was in sight; and neither were the dogs. I found a flight of steps in the thickness of the wall and went down them; and when I emerged again into the court, there stood the circle of dogs, the golden-brown one a little ahead of the others, the black greyhound shivering in the rear.

"Oh, hang it—you uncomfortable beasts, you!" I exclaimed, my voice startling me with a sudden echo. The dogs stood motionless, watching me. I knew by this time that they would not try to prevent my approaching the house, and the knowledge left me free to examine them. I had a feeling that they must be horribly cowed to be so silent and inert. Yet they did not look hungry or ill-treated. Their coats were smooth and they were not thin, except the shivering greyhound. It was more as if they had lived a long time with people who never spoke to them or looked at them: as though the silence of the place had gradually benumbed their busy inquisitive natures. And this strange passivity, this almost human lassitude, seemed to me sadder than the misery of starved and beaten animals. I should have liked to rouse them for a minute, to coax them into a game or a scamper; but the longer I looked into their fixed and weary eyes the more preposterous the idea became. With the windows of that house looking down on us, how could I have imagined such a thing? The dogs knew better: *they* knew what the house would tolerate and what it would not.

I even fancied that they knew what was passing through my mind, and pitied me for my frivolity. But even that feeling probably reached them through a thick fog of listlessness. I had an idea that their distance from me was as nothing to my remoteness from them. The impression they produced was that of having in common one memory so deep and dark that nothing that had happened since was worth either a growl or a wag.

"I say," I broke out abruptly, addressing myself to the dumb circle, "do you know what you look like, the whole lot of you? You look as if you'd seen a ghost—that's how you look! I wonder if there *is* a ghost here, and nobody but you left for it to appear to?" The dogs continued to gaze at me without moving....

It was dark when I saw Lanrivain's motor lamps at the cross-roads—and I wasn't exactly sorry to see them. I had the sense of having escaped from the loneliest place in the whole world, and of not liking loneliness—to that degree— as much as I had imagined I should. My friend had brought his solicitor back from Quimper for the night, and seated beside a fat and affable stranger I felt no inclination to talk of Kerfol....

But that evening, when Lanrivain and the solicitor were closeted in the study, Madame de Lanrivain began to question me in the drawing-room.

"Well—are you going to buy Kerfol?" she asked, tilting up her gay chin from her embroidery.

"I haven't decided yet. The fact is, I couldn't get into the house," I said, as if I had simply postponed my decision, and meant to go back for another look.

"You couldn't get in? Why, what happened? The family are mad to sell the place, and the old guardian has orders—"

"Very likely. But the old guardian wasn't there."

"What a pity! He must have gone to market. But his daughter—?"

"There was nobody about. At least I saw no one."

"How extraordinary! Literally nobody?"

"Nobody but a lot of dogs—a whole pack of them—who seemed to have the place to themselves."

Madame de Lanrivain let the embroidery slip to her knee and folded her hands on it. For several minutes she looked at me thoughtfully.

"A pack of dogs—you *saw* them?"

"Saw them? I saw nothing else!"

"How many?" She dropped her voice a little. "I've always wondered—"

I looked at her with surprise: I had supposed the place to be familiar to her. "Have you never been to Kerfol?" I asked.

"Oh, yes: often. But never on that day."

"What day?"

"I'd quite forgotten—and so had Hervé, I'm sure. If we'd remembered, we never should have sent you to-day—but then, after all, one doesn't half believe that sort of thing, does one?"

"What sort of thing?" I asked, involuntarily sinking my voice to the level of hers. Inwardly I was thinking: "I *knew* there was something...."

Madame de Lanrivain cleared her throat and produced a reassuring smile. "Didn't Hervé tell you the story of Kerfol? An ancestor of his was mixed up in it. You know every Breton house has its ghost-story; and some of them are rather unpleasant."

"Yes—but those dogs?"

"Well, those dogs are the ghosts of Kerfol. At least, the peasants say there's one day in the year when a lot of dogs appear there; and that day the keeper and his daughter go off to Morlaix and get drunk. The women in Brittany drink dreadfully." She stooped to match a silk; then she lifted her charming inquisitive Parisian face. "Did you *really* see a lot of dogs? There isn't one at Kerfol." she said.

II.

Lanrivain, the next day, hunted out a shabby calf volume from the back of an upper shelf of his library.

"Yes—here it is. What does it call itself? *A History of the Assizes of the Duchy of Brittany. Quimper, 1702.* The book was written about a hundred years later than the Kerfol affair; but I believe the account is transcribed pretty literally from the judicial records. Anyhow, it's queer reading. And there's a Hervé de Lanrivain mixed up in it—not exactly *my* style, as you'll see. But then he's only a collateral. Here, take the book up to bed with you. I don't exactly remember the details; but after you've read it I'll bet anything you'll leave your light burning all night!"

I left my light burning all night, as he had predicted; but it was chiefly because, till near dawn, I was absorbed in my reading. The account of the trial of Anne de Cornault, wife of the lord of Kerfol, was long and closely printed. It was, as my friend had said, probably an almost literal transcription of what took place in the court-room; and the trial lasted nearly a month. Besides, the type of the book was very bad....

At first I thought of translating the old record. But it is full of wearisome repetitions, and the main lines of the story are forever straying off into side issues. So I have tried to disentangle it, and give it here in a simpler form. At times, however, I have reverted to the text because no other words could have conveyed so exactly the sense of what I felt at Kerfol; and nowhere have I added anything of my own.

III.

It was in the year 16— that Yves de Cornault, lord of the domain of Kerfol, went to the *pardon* of Locronan to perform his religious duties. He was a rich and powerful noble, then in his sixty-second year, but hale and sturdy, a great horseman and hunter and a pious man. So all his neighbours attested. In appearance he was short and broad, with a swarthy face, legs slightly bowed from the saddle, a hanging nose and broad hands with black hairs on them. He had married young and lost his wife and son soon after, and since then had lived alone at Kerfol. Twice a year he went to Morlaix, where he had a handsome house by the river, and spent a week or ten days there; and occasionally he rode to Rennes on business. Witnesses were found to declare that during these absences he led a life different from the one he was known to lead at Kerfol, where he busied himself with his estate, attended mass daily, and found his only amusement in hunting the wild boar and water-fowl. But these rumours are not particularly relevant, and it is certain that among people of his own class in the neighbourhood he passed for a stern and even austere man, observant of his religious obligations, and keeping strictly to himself. There was no talk of any familiarity with the women on his estate, though at that time the nobility were very free with their peasants. Some people said he had never looked at a woman since his wife's death; but such things are hard to prove, and the evidence on this point was not worth much.

Well, in his sixty-second year, Yves de Cornault went to the *pardon* at Locronan, and saw there a young lady of Douarnenez, who had ridden over pillion behind her father to do her duty to the saint. Her name was Anne de Barrigan, and she came of good old Breton stock, but much less great and powerful than that of Yves de Cornault; and her father had squandered his fortune at cards, and lived almost like a peasant in his little granite manor on the moors.... I have said I would add nothing of my own to this bald statement of a strange case; but I must interrupt myself here to describe the young lady who rode up to the lych-gate of Locronan at the very moment when the Baron de Cornault was also dismounting there. I take my description from a faded drawing in red crayon, sober and truthful enough to be by a late pupil of the Clouets, which hangs in Lanrivain's study, and is said to be a portrait of Anne de Barrigan. It is unsigned and has no mark of identity but the initials A. B., and the date 16—, the year after her marriage. It represents a young woman with a small oval face, almost pointed, yet wide enough for a full mouth with a tender depression at the corners. The nose is small, and the eyebrows are set rather high, far apart, and as lightly pencilled as the eyebrows in a Chinese painting. The forehead is high and serious, and the hair, which one feels to be fine and thick and fair, is drawn off it and lies close like a cap. The eyes are neither large nor small, hazel probably, with a look at once shy and steady. A pair of beautiful long hands are crossed below the lady's breast....

The chaplain of Kerfol, and other witnesses, averred that when the Baron came back from Locronan he jumped from his horse, ordered another to be instantly saddled, called to a young page to come with him, and rode away that same evening to the south. His steward followed the next morning with coffers laden on a pair of pack mules. The following week Yves de Cornault rode back to Kerfol, sent for his vassals and tenants, and told them he was to be married at All Saints to Anne de Barrigan of Douarnenez. And on All Saints' Day the marriage took place.

As to the next few years, the evidence on both sides seems to show that they passed happily for the couple. No one was found to say that Yves de Cornault had been unkind to his wife, and it was plain to all that he was content with his bargain. Indeed, it was admitted by the chaplain and other witnesses for the prosecution that the young lady had a softening influence on her husband, and that he became less exacting with his tenants, less harsh to peasants and dependents, and less subject to the fits of gloomy silence which had darkened his widowhood. As to his wife, the only grievance her champions could call up in her behalf was that Kerfol was a lonely place, and that when her husband was away on business at Bennes or Morlaix—whither she was never taken—she was not allowed so much as to walk in the park unaccompanied. But no one asserted that she was unhappy, though one servant-woman said she had surprised her crying, and had heard her say that she was a woman accursed to have no child, and nothing in life to call her own. But that was a natural enough feeling in a wife attached to her husband; and certainly it must have been a great grief to Yves de Cornault that she bore no son. Yet he never made her feel her childlessness as a reproach—she admits this in her evidence—but seemed to try to make her forget it by showering gifts and favours on her. Rich though he was, he had never been openhanded; but nothing was too fine for his wife, in the way of silks or gems or linen, or whatever else she fancied. Every wandering merchant was welcome at Kerfol, and when the master was called away he never came back without bringing his wife a handsome present—something curious and particular—from Morlaix or Rennes or Quimper. One of the waiting-women gave, in cross-examination, an interesting list of one year's gifts, which I copy. From Morlaix, a carved ivory junk, with Chinamen at the oars, that a strange sailor had brought back as a votive offering for Notre Dame de la Clarté, above Ploumanac'h; from Quimper, an embroidered gown, worked by the nuns of the Assumption; from Rennes, a silver rose that opened and showed an amber Virgin with a crown of garnets; from

Morlaix, again, a length of Damascus velvet shot with gold, bought of a Jew from Syria; and for Michaelmas that same year, from Rennes, a necklet or bracelet of round stones— emeralds and pearls and rubies—strung like beads on a fine gold chain. This was the present that pleased the lady best, the woman said. Later on, as it happened, it was produced at the trial, and appears to have struck the Judges and the public as a curious and valuable jewel.

The very same winter, the Baron absented himself again, this time as far as Bordeaux, and on his return he brought his wife something even odder and prettier than the bracelet. It was a winter evening when he rode up to Kerfol and, walking into the hall, found her sitting by the hearth, her chin on her hand, looking into the fire. He carried a velvet box in his hand and, setting it down, lifted the lid and let out a little golden-brown dog.

Anne de Cornault exclaimed with pleasure as the little creature bounded toward her. "Oh, it looks like a bird or a butterfly!" she cried as she picked it up; and the dog put its paws on her shoulders and looked at her with eyes "like a Christian's." After that she would never have it out of her sight, and petted and talked to it as if it had been a child—as indeed it was the nearest thing to a child she was to know. Yves de Cornault was much pleased with his purchase. The dog had been brought to him by a sailor from an East India merchantman, and the sailor had bought it of a pilgrim in a bazaar at Jaffa, who had stolen it from a nobleman's wife in China: a perfectly permissible thing to do, since the pilgrim was a Christian and the nobleman a heathen doomed to hell-fire.

Yves de Cornault had paid a long price for the dog, for they were beginning to be in demand at the French court, and the sailor knew he had got hold of a good thing; but Anne's pleasure was so great that, to see her laugh and play with the little animal, her husband would doubtless have given twice the sum.

So far, all the evidence is at one, and the narrative plain sailing; but now the steering becomes difficult. I will try to keep as nearly as possible to Anne's own statements; though toward the end, poor thing....

Well, to go back. The very year after the little brown dog was brought to Kerfol, Yves de Cornault, one winter night, was found dead at the head of a narrow flight of stairs leading down from his wife's rooms to a door opening on the court. It was his wife who found him and gave the alarm, so distracted, poor wretch, with fear and horror—for his blood was all over her—that at first the roused household could not make out what she was saying, and thought she had suddenly gone mad. But there, sure enough, at the top of the stairs lay her husband, stone dead, and head foremost, the blood from his wounds dripping down to the steps below him. He had been dreadfully scratched and gashed about the face and throat, as if with curious pointed weapons; and one of his legs had a deep tear in it which had cut an artery, and probably caused his death. But how did he come there, and who had murdered him?

His wife declared that she had been asleep in her bed, and hearing his cry had rushed out to find him lying on the stairs; but this was immediately questioned. In the first place, it was proved that from her room she could not have heard the struggle on the stairs, owing to the thickness of the walls and the length of the intervening passage; then it was evident that she had not been in bed and asleep, since she was dressed when she roused the house, and her bed had not been slept in. Moreover, the door at the bottom of the stairs was ajar, and it was noticed by the chaplain (an observant man) that the dress she wore was stained with blood about the knees, and that there were traces of small blood-stained hands low down on the staircase walls, so that it was conjectured that she had really been at the postern-door when her husband fell and, feeling her way up to him in the darkness on her hands and knees, had been stained by his blood dripping down on her. Of course it was argued on the other side that the blood-marks on her dress might have been caused by her kneeling down by her husband when she rushed out of her room; but there was the open door below, and the fact that the finger-marks in the staircase all pointed upward.

The accused held to her statement for the first two days, in spite of its improbability; but on the third day word was brought to her that Hervé de Lanrivain, a young nobleman of the neighbourhood, had been arrested for complicity in the crime. Two or three witnesses thereupon came forward to say that it was known throughout the country that Lanrivain had formerly been on good terms with the lady of Cornault; but that he had been absent from Brittany for over a year, and people had ceased to associate their names. The witnesses who made this statement were not of a very reputable sort. One was an old herb-gatherer suspected of witchcraft, another a drunken clerk from a neighbouring parish, the third a half-witted shepherd who could be made to say anything; and it was clear that the prosecution was not satisfied with its case, and would have liked to find more definite proof of Lanrivain's complicity than the statement of the herb-gatherer, who swore to having seen him climbing the wall of the park on the night of the murder. One way of patching out incomplete proofs in those days was to put some sort of pressure, moral or physical, on the accused person. It is not clear what pressure was put on Anne de Cornault; but on the third day, when she was brought in court, she "appeared weak and wandering," and after being encouraged to collect herself and speak the truth, on her honour and the wounds of her Blessed Redeemer, she confessed that she had in fact gone down the stairs to speak with Hervé de Lanrivain (who denied everything), and had been surprised there by the sound of her husband's fall. That was better; and the prosecution rubbed its hands with satisfaction. The satisfaction increased when various dependents living at Kerfol were induced to say—with apparent sincerity—that during the year or two preceding his death their master had once more grown uncertain and irascible, and subject to the fits of brooding silence which his household had learned to dread before his second marriage. This seemed to show that things had not been going well at Kerfol; though no one could be found to say that there had been any signs of open disagreement between husband and wife.

Anne de Cornault, when questioned as to her reason for going down at night to open the door to Hervé de Lanrivain, made an answer which must have sent a smile around the court. She said it was because she was lonely and wanted to talk with the young man. Was this the only reason? she was asked; and replied: "Yes, by the Cross over your Lordships' heads." "But why at midnight?" the court asked. "Because I could see him in no other way." I can see the exchange of glances across the ermine collars under the Crucifix.

Anne de Cornault, further questioned, said that her married life had been extremely lonely: "desolate" was the word she used. It was true that her husband seldom spoke harshly to her; but there were days when he did not speak at all. It was true that he had never struck or threatened her; but he kept her like a prisoner at Kerfol, and when he rode away to Morlaix or Quimper or Rennes he set so close a watch on her that she could not pick a flower in the garden without having a waiting-woman at her heels. "I am no Queen, to need such honours," she once said to him; and he had answered that a man who has a treasure does not leave the key in the lock when he goes out. "Then take me with you," she urged; but to this he said that towns were pernicious places, and young wives better off at their own firesides.

"But what did you want to say to Hervé de Lanrivain?" the court asked; and she answered: "To ask him to take me away."

"Ah—you confess that you went down to him with adulterous thoughts?"

"Then why did you want him to take you away?"

"Because I was afraid for my life."

"Of whom were you afraid?"

"Of my husband."

"Why were you afraid of your husband?"

"Because he had strangled my little dog."

Another smile must have passed around the courtroom: in days when any nobleman had a right to hang his peasants—and most of them exercised it—pinching a pet animal's wind-pipe was nothing to make a fuss about.

At this point one of the Judges, who appears to have had a certain sympathy for the accused, suggested that she should be allowed to explain herself in her own way; and she thereupon made the following statement.

The first years of her marriage had been lonely; but her husband had not been unkind to her. If she had had a child she would not have been unhappy; but the days were long, and it rained too much.

It was true that her husband, whenever he went away and left her, brought her a handsome present on his return; but this did not make up for the loneliness. At least nothing had, till he brought her the little brown dog from the East: after that she was much less unhappy. Her husband seemed pleased that she was so fond of the dog; he gave her leave to put her jewelled bracelet around its neck, and to keep it always with her.

One day she had fallen asleep in her room, with the dog at her feet, as his habit was. Her feet were bare and resting on his back. Suddenly she was waked by her husband: he stood beside her, smiling not unkindly.

"You look like my great-grandmother, Juliane de Cornault, lying in the chapel with her feet on a little dog," he said.

The analogy sent a chill through her, but she laughed and answered: "Well, when I am dead you must put me beside her, carved in marble, with my dog at my feet."

"Oho—we'll wait and see," he said, laughing also, but

with his black brows close together. "The dog is the emblem of fidelity."

"And do you doubt my right to lie with mine at my feet?"

"When I'm in doubt I find out," he answered. "I am an old man," he added, "and people say I make you lead a lonely life. But I swear you shall have your monument if you earn it."

"And I swear to be faithful," she returned, "if only for the sake of having my little dog at my feet."

Not long afterward he went on business to the Quimper Assizes; and while he was away his aunt, the widow of a great nobleman of the duchy, came to spend a night at Kerfol on her way to the *pardon* of Ste. Barbe. She was a woman of piety and consequence, and much respected by Yves de Cornault, and when she proposed to Anne to go with her to Ste. Barbe no one could object, and even the chaplain declared himself in favour of the pilgrimage. So Anne set out for Ste. Barbe, and there for the first time she talked with Hervé de Lanrivain. He had come once or twice to Kerfol with his father, but she had never before exchanged a dozen words with him. They did not talk for more than five minutes now: it was under the chestnuts, as the procession was coming out of the chapel. He said: "I pity you," and she was surprised, for she had not supposed that any one thought her an object of pity. He added: "Call for me when you need me," and she smiled a little, but was glad afterward, and thought often of the meeting.

She confessed to having seen him three times afterward: not more. How or where she would not say—one had the impression that she feared to implicate some one. Their meetings had been rare and brief; and at the last he had told her that he was starting the next day for a foreign country, on a mission which was not without peril and might keep him for many months absent. He asked her for a remembrance, and she had none to give him but the collar about the little dog's neck. She was sorry afterward that she had given it, but he was so unhappy at going that she had not had the courage to refuse.

Her husband was away at the time. When he returned a few days later he picked up the animal to pet it, and noticed that its collar was missing. His wife told him that the dog had lost it in the undergrowth of the park, and that she and her maids had hunted a whole day for it. It was true, she explained to the court, that she had made the maids search for the necklet—they all believed the dog had lost it in the park....

Her husband made no comment, and that evening at supper he was in his usual mood, between good and bad: you could never tell which. He talked a good deal, describing what he had seen and done at Rennes; but now and then he stopped and looked hard at her, and when she went to bed she found her little dog strangled on her pillow. The little thing was dead, but still warm; she stooped to lift it, and her distress turned to horror when she discovered that it had been strangled by twisting twice round its throat the necklet she had given to Lanrivain.

The next morning at dawn she buried the dog in the garden, and hid the necklet in her breast. She said nothing to her husband, then or later, and he said nothing to her; but that day he had a peasant hanged for stealing a faggot in the park, and the next day he nearly beat to death a young horse he was breaking.

Winter set in, and the short days passed, and the long nights, one by one; and she heard nothing of Hervé de Lanrivain. It might be that her husband had killed him; or merely that he had been robbed of the necklet. Day after day by the hearth among the spinning maids, night after night alone on her bed, she wondered and trembled. Sometimes at table her husband looked across at her and smiled; and then she felt sure that Lanrivain was dead. She dared not try to get news of him, for she was sure her husband would find out if she did: she had an idea that he could find out anything. Even when a witchwoman who was a noted seer, and could show you the whole world in her crystal, came to the castle for a night's shelter, and the maids flocked to her, Anne held back.

The winter was long and black and rainy. One day, in Yves de Cornault's absence, some gypsies came to Kerfol with a troop of performing dogs. Anne bought the smallest and cleverest, a white dog with a feathery coat and one blue and one brown eye. It seemed to have been ill-treated by the gypsies, and clung to her plaintively when she took it from them. That evening her husband came back, and when she went to bed she found the dog strangled on her pillow.

After that she said to herself that she would never have another dog; but one bitter cold evening a poor lean greyhound was found whining at the castle-gate, and she took him in and forbade the maids to speak of him to her husband. She hid him in a room that no one went to, smuggled food to him from her own plate, made him a warm bed to lie on and petted him like a child.

Yves de Cornault came home, and the next day she found the greyhound strangled on her pillow. She wept in secret, but said nothing, and resolved that even if she met a dog dying of hunger she would never bring him into the castle; but one day she found a young sheepdog, a brindled puppy with good blue eyes, lying with a broken leg in the snow of the park. Yves de Cornault was at Bennes, and she brought the dog in, warmed and fed it, tied up its leg and hid it in the castle till her husband's return. The day before, she gave it to a peasant woman who lived a long way off, and paid her handsomely to care for it and say nothing; but that night she heard a whining and scratching at her door, and when she opened it the lame puppy, drenched and shivering, jumped up on her with little sobbing barks. She hid him in her bed, and the next morning was about to have him taken back to the peasant woman when she heard her husband ride into the court. She shut the dog in a chest, and went down to receive him. An hour or two later, when she returned to her room, the puppy lay strangled on her pillow....

After that she dared not make a pet of any other dog; and her loneliness became almost unendurable. Sometimes, when she crossed the court of the castle, and thought no one was looking, she stopped to pat the old pointer at the gate. But one day as she was caressing him her husband came out of the chapel; and the next day the old dog was gone....

This curious narrative was not told in one sitting of the court, or received without impatience and incredulous comment. It was plain that the Judges were surprised by its puerility, and that it did not help the accused in the eyes of the public. It was an odd tale, certainly; but what did it prove? That Yves de Cornault disliked dogs, and that his wife, to gratify her own fancy, persistently ignored this dislike. As for pleading this trivial disagreement as an excuse for her relations—whatever their nature—with her supposed accomplice, the argument was so absurd that her own lawyer manifestly regretted having let her make use of it, and tried several times to cut short her story. But she went on to the end, with a kind of hypnotized insistence, as though the scenes she evoked were so real to her that she had forgotten where she was and imagined herself to be re-living them.

At length the Judge who had previously shown a certain kindness to her said (leaning forward a little, one may suppose, from his row of dozing colleagues): "Then you would have us believe that you murdered your husband because he would not let you keep a pet dog?"

"I did not murder my husband."

"Who did, then? Hervé de Lanrivain?"

"No."

"Who then? Can you tell us?"

"Yes, I can tell you. The dogs—" At that point she was carried out of the court in a swoon.

It was evident that her lawyer tried to get her to abandon this line of defense. Possibly her explanation, whatever it was, had seemed convincing when she poured it out to him in the heat of their first private colloquy; but now that it was exposed to the cold daylight of judicial scrutiny, and the banter of the town, he was thoroughly ashamed of it, and would have sacrificed her without a scruple to save his professional reputation. But the obstinate Judge—who perhaps, after all, was more inquisitive than kindly—evidently wanted to hear the story out, and she was ordered, the next day, to continue her deposition.

She said that after the disappearance of the old watchdog nothing particular happened for a month or two. Her husband was much as usual: she did not remember any special incident. But one evening a pedlar woman came to the castle and was selling trinkets to the maids. She had no heart for trinkets, but she stood looking on while the women made their choice. And then, she did not know how, but the pedlar coaxed her into buying for herself a pear-shaped pomander with a strong scent in it—she had once seen something of the kind on a gypsy woman. She had no desire for the pomander, and did not know why she had bought it. The pedlar said that whoever wore it had the power to read the future; but she did not really believe that, or care much either. However, she bought the thing and took it up to her room, where she sat turning it about in her hand. Then the strange scent attracted her and she began to wonder what kind of spice was in the box. She opened it and found a grey bean rolled in a strip of paper; and on the paper she saw a sign she knew, and a message from Hervé de Lanrivain, saying that he was at home again and would be at the door in the court that night after the moon had set....

She burned the paper and sat down to think. It was nightfall, and her husband was at home.... She had no way of warning Lanrivain, and there was nothing to do but to wait....

At this point I fancy the drowsy court-room beginning to wake up. Even to the oldest hand on the bench there must have been a certain relish in picturing the feelings of a woman on receiving such a message at nightfall from a man living twenty miles away, to whom she had no means of sending a warning....

She was not a clever woman, I imagine; and as the first result of her cogitation she appears to have made the mistake of being, that evening, too kind to her husband. She could not ply him with wine, according to the traditional expedient, for though he drank heavily at times he had a strong head; and when he drank beyond its strength it was because he chose to, and not because a woman coaxed him. Not his wife, at any rate—she was an old story by now. As I read the case, I fancy there was no feeling for her left in him but the hatred occasioned by his supposed dishonour.

At any rate, she tried to call up her old graces; but early in the evening he complained of pains and fever, and left the hall to go up to the closet where he sometimes slept. His servant carried him a cup of hot wine, and brought back word that he was sleeping and not to be disturbed; and an hour later, when Anne lifted the tapestry and listened at his door, she heard his loud regular breathing. She thought it might be a feint, and stayed a long time barefooted in the passage, her ear to the crack; but the breathing went on too steadily and naturally to be other than that of a man in a sound sleep. She crept back to her room reassured, and stood in the window watching the moon set through the trees of the park. The sky was misty and starless, and after the moon went down the night was black as pitch. She knew the time had come, and stole along the passage, past her husband's door—where she stopped again to listen to his breathing—to the top of the stairs. There she paused a moment, and assured herself that no one was following her; then she began to go down the stairs in the darkness. They were so steep and winding that she had to go very slowly, for fear of stumbling. Her one thought was to get the door unbolted, tell Lanrivain to make his escape, and hasten back to her room. She had tried the bolt earlier in the evening, and managed to put a little grease on it; but nevertheless, when she drew it, it gave a squeak... not loud, but it made her heart stop; and the next minute, overhead, she heard a noise....

"What noise?" the prosecution interposed.

"My husband's voice calling out my name and cursing me."

"What did you hear after that?"

"A terrible scream and a fall."

"Where was Hervé de Lanrivain at this time?"

"He was standing outside in the court. I just made him out in the darkness. I told him for God's sake to go, and then I pushed the door shut."

"What did you do next?"

"I stood at the foot of the stairs and listened."

"What did you hear?"

"I heard dogs snarling and panting." (Visible discouragement of the bench, boredom of the public, and exasperation of the lawyer for the defense. Dogs again—! But the inquisitive Judge insisted.)

"What dogs?"

She bent her head and spoke so low that she had to be told to repeat her answer: "I don't know."

"How do you mean—you don't know?"

"I don't know what dogs...."

The Judge again intervened: "Try to tell us exactly what happened. How long did you remain at the foot of the stairs?"

"Only a few minutes."

"And what was going on meanwhile overhead?"

"The dogs kept on snarling and panting. Once or twice he cried out. I think he moaned once. Then he was quiet."

"Then what happened?"

"Then I heard a sound like the noise of a pack when the wolf is thrown to them—gulping and lapping."

(There was a groan of disgust and repulsion through the court, and another attempted intervention by the distracted lawyer. But the inquisitive Judge was still inquisitive.)

"And all the while you did not go up?"

"Yes—I went up then—to drive them off."

"The dogs?"

"Yes."

"Well—?"

"When I got there it was quite dark. I found my husband's flint and steel and struck a spark. I saw him lying there. He was dead."

"And the dogs?"

"The dogs were gone."

"Gone—whereto?"

"I don't know. There was no way out—and there were no dogs at Kerfol."

She straightened herself to her full height, threw her arms above her head, and fell down on the stone floor with a long scream. There was a moment of confusion in the court-room. Some one on the bench was heard to say: "This is clearly a case for the ecclesiastical authorities"—and the prisoner's lawyer doubtless jumped at the suggestion.

After this, the trial loses itself in a maze of cross-questioning and squabbling. Every witness who was called corroborated Anne de Cornault's statement that there were no dogs at Kerfol: had been none for several months. The master of the house had taken a dislike to dogs, there was no denying it But, on the other hand, at the inquest, there had been long and bitter discussions as to the nature of the dead man's wounds. One of the surgeons called in had spoken of marks that looked like bites. The suggestion of witchcraft was revived, and the opposing lawyers hurled tomes of necromancy at each other.

At last Anne de Cornault was brought back into court—

at the instance of the same Judge—and asked if she knew where the dogs she spoke of could have come from. On the body of her Redeemer she swore that she did not. Then the Judge put his final question: "If the dogs you think you heard had been known to you, do you think you would have recognized them by their barking?"

"Yes."

"Did you recognize them?"

"Yes."

"What dogs do you take them to have been?"

"My dead dogs," she said in a whisper…. She was taken out of court, not to reappear there again. There was some kind of ecclesiastical investigation, and the end of the business was that the Judges disagreed with each other, and with the ecclesiastical committee, and that

Anne de Cornault was finally handed over to the keeping of her husband's family, who shut her up in the keep of Kerfol, where she is said to have died many years later, a harmless mad-woman.

So ends her story. As for that of Hervé de Lanrivain, I had only to apply to his collateral descendant for its subsequent details. The evidence against the young man being insufficient, and his family influence in the duchy considerable, he was set free, and left soon afterward for Paris. He was probably in no mood for a worldly life, and he appears to have come almost immediately under the influence of the famous M.

Arnauld d'Andilly and the gentlemen of Port Royal. A year
or two later he was received into their Order, and without
achieving any particular distinction he followed its good and
evil fortunes till his death some twenty years later. Lanrivain
showed me a portrait of him by a pupil of Philippe de
Champaigne: sad eyes, an impulsive mouth and a narrow
brow. Poor Hervé de Lanrivain: it was a grey ending. Yet
as I looked at his stiff and sallow effigy, in the dark dress of
the Janséniste, I almost found myself envying his fate. After
all, in the course of his life two great things had happened
to him: he had loved romantically, and he must have talked
with Pascal....